D0251298

Angel Bites the Bullet

Angel
Bites the Bullet

JUDY DELTON

Illustrated by Jill Weber

Houghton Mifflin Company
Boston 2000

Copyright © 2000 by Judy Delton
Illustrations copyright © 2000 by Jill Weber

All rights reserved. For information about permission to
reproduce selections from this book, write to Permissions,
Houghton Mifflin Company, 215 Park Avenue South,
New York, New York 10003.

www.hmco.com/trade

The text of this book is set in 12-point Stone Serif.

Library of Congress Cataloging-in-Publication Data

Delton, Judy.
Angel bites the bullet / Judy Delton; illustrated by Jill Weber.
p.   cm.
Summary: Angel and her best friend try to find a way
to get rid of the well-meaning, but disaster-prone family
friend who has moved into Angel's bedroom.
ISBN 0-618-04085-4
[1. Worry—Fiction. 2. Family life—Fiction.
3. Friendship—Fiction.] I. Weber, Jill, ill. II. Title.
PZ7.D388Am   2000
[Fic]—dc21
00-027600

Manufactured in the United States of America
HAD 10 9 8 7 6 5 4 3 2 1

For Amy Flynn,
who understands what a worrywart Angel is.

For Kate DiCamillo,
who is Flannery O'Connor without the peacocks.

For Rosalie Maggio,
a sui generis of the billet-doux, the book,
and the bergamot.

For my workshop scribes
who fill my atelier with esprit de corps.

CONTENTS

ONE

The Eye of the Storm

"My name is Bert and I dig in the dirt," sang Rags from under the front porch. His name was not Bert but Theodore. He wished it were Bert, so he often pretended it was. It was his favorite name. His mother told him it was very creative of him to have an imaginary name, and also to make up rhymes about things. So Rags made up rhymes a lot.

His sister Angel could hear him under the front porch of their big green house in Elm City, Wisconsin, where she sat in the swing, reading.

She had a new book, called *The Mystery of the Haunted Villa,* and some Greek lemon bars to eat. Rags had created a whole small city under the porch, with tiny lakes and stick trees and matchbox cars and matchbox houses. His mother said she was afraid the house would fall from all the digging, but so far it hadn't.

Angel had a baby sister too, called Athena, who was taking a morning nap. Angel felt very peaceful because at the moment she had no worries. She thought she could come up with some worries if she tried very hard, but right now she felt like purring like a kitten. The family had returned from a trip to Greece, Angel was in her own safe home again, and all her worries were over. Her mother's friend Alyce, who had rented the house while they were gone, was back in her own apartment, and the repairmen had fixed the pipes and all the other things in Angel's house that had broken in their absence. Alyce meant well, but things seemed to go awry when she was in charge.

"She's a good person, Angel," said Mrs. Poppadopolis. "She has a heart of gold. It's not her fault that she is accident-prone."

Well, all that was behind them. There would be no new surprises. In another month school would be starting, and in the meantime she and her best friend, Edna, had books to read, bikes to ride, picnics to pack, and news to catch up on. And Rudy, Angel's stepfather, had just painted the walls of her bedroom blue and white to remind her of Greece: the blue of the sea and the white of the hillside homes. Surely he would not have bothered unless they were to stay in one place for a while — Elm City.

Rudy said that Angel was so grown-up now (having recovered bravely from her fear of travel) that she should be called by her real name, Caroline, instead of her nickname, Angel. But so far, he was the only one who remembered it.

"Caroline," he would say, "let's have a game of checkers." Or "Caroline, maybe you could use some new white curtains for your bedroom."

There was no doubt about it, Rudy was a wonderful father. It was hard to remember life without him.

Angel felt the warm almost-autumn sun on her hair, listened to the scrunch, scrunch, scrunch of Rags's shovel in the dirt, and dozed off in the porch swing. Her book fell to the floor. She dreamed about the little Greek village where her new grandparents lived, with the dusty roads and grazing goats. It was pleasant to dream about the trip to Greece, now that she was safely back home. The danger was over.

The church bells rang, and for a minute Angel thought she was really back in Greece. But then a horn honked and broke the silence. Angel woke up. A car pulled to the curb. It was Alyce's car, and Alyce was behind the wheel. Angel's stomach muscles tightened, and she felt her eye twitch. Lately her eye twitched if there was trouble nearby.

But of course that was silly. Alyce probably had just forgotten a pincushion or some cat food or birdseed and had come to collect it.

Alyce waved. Angel's eye twitched again. Alyce ran up the back steps as if she had a mission. Something was on her mind. She had a shopping bag in her hand. Not a new shopping bag as if she had just bought a new dress she wanted to show Angel's mom, but an old shopping bag, which meant she had something from home that she was bringing to Angel's. Angel frowned. She should be taking things out, not bringing them in!

Rags crawled out from under the porch and went inside the house. Now there was loud talk coming from the kitchen. Talk that sounded like emergency talk. But all the emergencies were over. Alyce had moved out and all the damage had been repaired.

Angel tried to read again, but her attention wandered. And then the front door burst open and Rags came tumbling out, shouting, "Hey, guess what? Alyce is moving back in with us! She gets to share your room. Bubba's coming too, isn't that great?"

Bubba was Alyce's sheepdog. He shed. He had

just left. No, it was not great. No way was Alyce (or Bubba) going to move into her little blue and white room!

Now Angel knew that her tight stomach and her twitching eye were omens, warning her of what was to come.

TWO

Thunder

Alyce came out on the porch wiping her eyes. Angel's mother had her arm around Alyce and was saying, "There, there, it will all work out." Mrs. Poppadopolis always smiled (especially since the pipes had been fixed), but now she was frowning. She looked as if any minute she would cry along with Alyce.

"I won't be a bit of trouble," sobbed Alyce. "It will be as if I never left. And my living here worked out so well, it was like—practice."

Practice? Her renting the house had been *practice?*

"There's been a little problem at her apartment, Angel," said Mrs. Poppadopolis. She did not explain what had happened, and Angel did not ask.

"Alyce needs a helping hand while they do repairs," her mother went on.

But why our helping hand? Angel wanted to ask. But she didn't.

"You won't know I'm here," sniffed Alyce. "I'll be as quiet as a mouse in your other twin bed, Angel. And before long, *poof!* I'll be gone!"

Oh, if only Angel could believe that! And *poof* didn't sound like a word she wanted to hear from Alyce. *Poof* meant smoke, and smoke meant fire.

Alyce went to the car to get the things she had just moved out. One by one the family watched her move her dress form, bird cage, and pet food back in.

"Bubba could have died," she said. "I'm so lucky I have somewhere to go, someone to turn to."

Alyce drove off to get more things, and her

mother put her arm around Angel. "I couldn't tell her to go to a hotel, Angel," she said. "She can't afford it, and we can't put her out on the street."

"Doesn't she have other friends?" asked Angel.

"They all have apartments smaller than hers. Let's just bite the bullet and be brave."

Angel was tired of being brave. She was tired of being unselfish and grown-up about things. She was tired of Alyce, period. She didn't care if no one called her Caroline. She'd be called Angel forever, because she didn't ever want to grow up and bite bullets.

Athena began to cry. Rags began to pout. Mrs. Poppadopolis began to scrub the sink, which was what she always did when there was trouble. Now she was scrubbing it so hard that Angel worried the finish would wear off.

Suddenly the sun went behind a cloud and a clap of thunder sounded. It began to rain. Angel ran out to get her book, which was wet. This was not a good sign, thought Angel.

And then through the rain, wearing her yellow slicker and riding her bike, came Edna. Well, that was a spot of hope, thought Angel. She still had a best friend, anyway. With Angel's luck, Edna would ride right by and go to someone else's house. But she didn't. She parked her bike at the fence and ran up the steps.

Angel wanted to spill out the bad news to her friend right away. She wanted Edna to feel sorry for her. She wanted Edna to solve the problem and get rid of Alyce before she even had a chance to move in. Edna often solved problems. She was very smart.

"I heard the news," were Edna's first words. "Alyce is moving back in. What a bummer."

Angel didn't even have a chance to complain. To tell the bad news. It was all over town already!

"I guess the fire wasn't her fault," said Edna. "At least that's what the fireman said."

"Fire?" said Angel.

"She turned the grill down low," said Edna, "but it was too late. And when Bubba knocked it off the table — well, the rest, as they say, is history."

"She was grilling in the house?" shouted Angel.

Edna nodded. "A tofu pork chop," she said.

"Isn't that dangerous?"

12

"Obviously it was," said Edna sensibly. "Her landlord was lucky the whole building didn't go up in flames. The firemen worked hard to contain it to the one floor. But that place is totaled."

Angel was pretty sure the landlord did not feel lucky about anything. Especially to have Alyce as a tenant.

By noon Alyce had re-moved in with the Poppadopolises.

The rain stopped, and Angel turned to Edna and said, "I need help. We have to get my room back."

"I have an idea," said Edna.

Now those were the words Angel wanted to hear. Her stomach settled down. Edna's idea would solve the problem. And the sooner the better.

But where could they talk? Angel already had no privacy. Alyce was already hanging her pant-suits in Angel's blue and white closet.

"Let's go to my house," said Edna.

Angel got her bike out of the garage and the girls were off.

"Welcome home from Greece!" said Edna's mother to Angel as the girls ran through the kitchen. "Did you have a good time?"

"Yes, thank you," said Angel. It seemed ages ago that she had gone to Greece. Ages ago since her worries were only about plane crashes and eating fish heads. Now she had *real* worries.

When the girls got to Edna's room, Edna closed the door and locked it. How lucky Edna was to have her own room! And to have a lock on the door! No one would ever bother her. No Rags whimpering and whining to get in. No Alyce with her pantyhose in Angel's drawers.

Edna got her notebook from her desk drawer. She got her new red gel-flow pen. "Now," she said. "Let's talk business."

THREE

Lightning

"You want Alyce out, right?" said Edna.

Angel nodded her head vigorously. She felt a little guilty and selfish for feeling this way, but she was up to her ears with Alyce.

"I thought this would be a problem," said Edna thoughtfully. "Last night I was watching a movie on TV and an idea hit me like a flash of lightning!"

Angel watched TV movies too, and lightning never struck.

"Now, first I'll mention some options," said

Edna. "Some things to think about before we do anything drastic. We have to write them down."

Angel wasn't sure what options were, but if Edna said they should be put down, they had to be put down. If an option could get rid of Alyce, it was a good thing, no matter what it meant.

"I'm using my red pen," said Edna, "because red means it's important. Now the most obvious thing to do would be to ask her to leave. Tell her you want your privacy. You don't want to share your room."

"That's not polite," said Angel. "And my mom wouldn't like it. She said she could stay."

Edna didn't have much truck with politeness.

"Well, it probably wouldn't work. It didn't work in the movie. Alyce won't go that easily," said Edna. "She's hard to move, once she digs in, so to speak. We have to find a good reason to make her leave. Something not so obvious. Like somebody sends her on a cruise or something. That was one of the options in this movie."

"Cruises cost money," said Angel. "Lots of money."

"Right," said Edna. "We need to find something that will make her *want* to move out, something that doesn't cost money. And what makes people want to have their own place?"

Angel wondered what Edna was getting at. She couldn't think of a thing that would make Alyce move out.

"A husband!" said Edna. "A husband would be a permanent solution! We wouldn't have to worry about this happening again."

Of all of Edna's ideas, that was the last one Angel would have thought of.

"If we don't do something drastic," added Edna, "she'll come back and back like a bad penny. The only way to get rid of her for good is a husband. Women will do anything for husbands."

"Alyce doesn't have a husband," said Angel.

"Duh," said Edna. "That's the whole point! It's up to us to find her one. A rich one who

could pay the rent! Then she'd move out fast. It's the perfect answer."

If this was what Edna called an option, she must be losing her touch, thought Angel.

"Even if she did have a husband, she'd probably just keep living with us," said Angel. "The husband would move in too, just like Bubba."

Now Angel could see a bald man with a cane on a little cot that her parents had put between her two twin beds. It was a tight fit. And where would he keep his clothes and golf clubs and shaving supplies?

Edna looked pained. "No, no, no." She sighed. "No married couple would want to live in a house with three children and two adults."

"Why not?" asked Angel. "Alyce loves our house."

"She may love it now," said Edna, "but she wouldn't love it if she had a husband. When you have a husband, you want to be alone."

"My mom has a husband and she isn't alone," said Angel.

Edna put her head down on her desk and

banged it three times. "When you first get married, you want to be alone. Take my word for it," she said.

Angel hated to argue with Edna, but her own parents had not been alone when they got married. They had been with Angel and Rags.

Edna looked at her and said clearly, "Pri-va-cy. Get it?"

Angel got it. But would Alyce?

"Alyce probably doesn't know about that," she said.

"She knows, trust me," said Edna. "Let's just concentrate on how we find the right guy as fast as we can. We need to get this show on the road."

"Maybe Alyce doesn't want a husband," said Angel. "Not everyone wants to be married."

"Alyce is the marrying kind, trust me. She'll thank us," said Edna. "My mom says every woman secretly wants a husband. The guy we find will be so great she'll fall head over heels in love with him and be grateful to us for finding him."

Angel began to be hopeful. Edna did not usually make mistakes. After all, she had staged their house so that it would rent when they went to Greece. Well, she did get the wrong renter, but her idea was sound. And she actually was an expert on the birds and the bees. She knew all about babies when Athena was born. Things Angel did not know.

"A husband is really drastic," said Angel.

Edna nodded. "It's the only thing that will get her out," said Edna. "Something really drastic. I think the failure factor on this one is almost zero."

Angel was definitely in favor of something that would not fail.

"What do we do first?" she asked Edna.

Edna looked pleased that Angel was on the bandwagon. "Well, my cousin in Denver put one of those ads in the paper, you know, 'man wanted' ads."

Rudy had looked in the newspaper when he wanted a car and someone to mow the lawn. Her mother had looked in the ads for babysitters when Angel was smaller. But she had never heard of looking for a husband the way you looked for a plumber or roofer.

"Did your cousin find a husband?" asked Angel.

Edna nodded. "She did, but it didn't work out. He had another wife in Ohio."

Angel looked shocked. Even Angel knew people were allowed only one husband or wife at a time.

"The other option," said Edna, moving on to a safer subject, "is a blind date. We look around and find someone and arrange for them to go out together on a date. We have to find someone with Alyce's interests, that's important. So they have stuff in common."

There was that word again, *option.*

"Does she have any interests, Angel?" asked Edna doubtfully.

"Pets, I guess. And gardening."

"Does she read books?" demanded Edna.

"Magazines," said Angel. "Pet magazines, and

brides' magazines, and movie magazines, and *TV Times*. And some sewing magazines."

"Aha! Brides! I told you she wanted a husband! You can't be a bride without a man. We'd better get started. Every moment we delay is a moment longer in your bedroom!"

Angel jumped to her feet. Edna was right. There was no time to lose.

"Which one should we try first?" she said.

"Let's do both," said Edna, who was a strong believer in having your cake and eating it too. "We'll look at the ads in the paper, and at the same time we will keep our eyes open for a blind date."

Edna's mother called her for lunch.

"Let's start this afternoon," said Edna. "Maybe we can go to the park and sit at a picnic table. I'll bring a newspaper and some lemonade."

Angel got on her bike and rode home. When she got to her yard, she smelled something burning. She hoped it wasn't the house. Alyce definitely had a problem with fire.

FOUR

The Other Shoe

"Alyce made your lunch, dear!" said her mother, overly brightly, it seemed. Her mother appeared to be in a cloud of smoke. The cloud filled the kitchen. Rags was eating peanut butter on a bagel.

"You can scrape the black off the hot dogs with no trouble," said Alyce cheerfully.

Angel wondered why her mother let Alyce near the stove. That was the reason she was there in the first place — the barbecue fiasco.

"Cooking for my little family is the least I can

do for my keep," said Alyce, answering Angel's unasked question. "I like to pay my way."

Edna was right. Alyce did need a husband. Even some children. Someone of her own to burn food for.

"Burned hot dogs are good!" said Rags, putting one on his peanut butter bagel. "I hope you stay a long time and make all our dinners!"

Angel glared at Rags. She wanted to clap her hand over his mouth. Saying those words was worse than swearing. It was obvious that Rags did not have to share his room with panty-hose and dress forms and canaries and skin care products. All he had to do was eat Alyce's burned food. And he even *liked* it! He was home free! It was Angel who was paying the toll.

"Bert likes burned dogs better than frogs!" sang Rags. When no one noticed his rhyme, he sang it again.

"Nice, Rags," said his mother finally.

"I'm going to the park," said Angel, putting her plate in the sink.

Athena reached out her little arms to Angel, asking Angel to take her along. "Park!" she said.

"I can't take you today," said Angel, feeling guilty for the second time that day. "Edna and I have this . . . project to do."

"Hey, school's out. There aren't no projects in summer!" said Rags.

"Any," said his mother. "There aren't *any* projects in the summer."

"I know it!" said Rags. "That's what I said! Tell Angel!"

"I'll be glad to take Thena to the park," said Alyce, who was already through washing the dishes in cold water and was drying them with something that looked like Rags's blanket. "I love to go to the park with the other mothers!"

What was the matter with this picture? Angel wanted to ask Alyce. Well, Alyce wasn't one of "the other mothers," for one thing! Now Angel would not even be Alyce-less in the park. Alyce was everywhere. She was ubiquitous, like Superman! Well, at least she was sure she and Edna were on the right track. Marriage and mother-hood were just what the doctor had ordered. If Alyce had a real baby of her own, she would be a real mother and wouldn't have to borrow other people's babies.

Angel hopped on her bike and Alyce put Thena in the stroller.

"Wait for me!" she called to Angel. But Angel was off like a shot and on the way to Edna's house.

"We need another place to meet," she said to Edna, breathing hard from hurrying. "Alyce is going to the park with Thena."

"The park is huge," said Edna, waving Angel's words away.

"She'll find us," said Angel. "She'll find us right away."

"Alyce is driving you crazy," said Edna. "We have to act fast. You could have a nervous breakdown, like my great-aunt Martha."

Edna was right. Angel had to get a grip on her-self. She wasn't being pursued. Or stalked. Yet.

But when they got to the park, it wasn't Alyce who found them. It was Rudy! He was with another clown from the TV show he did, named Janet. They were laughing.

"It was so nice out today," he said, "we thought we'd take our break in the park. The studio is right across the street."

Angel knew where the studio was. Why did Rudy explain it? And why was he with Janet, laughing and talking? She supposed clowns naturally liked to laugh. She was letting her imagination get away from her again. It was perfectly natural to take a break in the park. With another clown.

"See you tonight, Angel!" he said, waving.

Edna frowned. "Why was he with Janet?" she said.

"He works with her!" said Angel. "It's the most natural thing in the world."

"Maybe," said Edna. "But I wonder if he doesn't like to . . . you know, delay going home, with Alyce there all the time talking away and

burning food. And not having any *p-r-i-v-a-c-y.*"

"That is not true!" said Angel stamping her foot. "We have a big house! He has lots of privacy!"

"I guess," said Edna, getting out her notebook. "I'm just waiting for the other shoe to drop."

What did Edna mean? What other shoe? Angel saw her problems piling up. First there was Alyce moving back in. Then there was Rudy in the park with Janet. And now, even she and her best friend, Edna, were beginning to fight! Where would all this end?

"Okay," said Edna, brushing some ants off the picnic table and wiping up someone's spilled ketchup with a tissue. "Why don't people use a tablecloth when they have a picnic? We always do."

Rudy was just on a break, for heaven's sake. It wasn't as if he met Janet for dinner every night and didn't come home at all. Her imagination was running away with her. How many times had this happened? Edna didn't know *everything.*

All of a sudden Rudy and Janet came running by on the way back to the office. "Oh, Angel," called Rudy, throwing paper wrappers from their doughnuts in the trash barrel. "Could you tell Mom I'll be a little late tonight? We've got a meeting after work, but keep my dinner hot!"

Janet nodded. "It won't be a long meeting." She laughed.

"Okay," said Angel. "I'll tell her."

There was Edna's other shoe. The meeting was the other shoe. And it had just dropped.

FIVE

Mr. Right

"I don't know about you," said Edna suspiciously, "but I think things look pretty grim. Janet seems to have her eye on Rudy. I think Alyce is wrecking your family. We'd better work fast."

Angel began to feel angry with Edna. Couldn't she see that this was just her imagination? Still, if Edna saw trouble, maybe it wasn't her imagination. Edna was known for facts, and getting things right. When her mother sent her to the store, she didn't even have to make a list. Edna knew what was needed, and what brand was the best buy.

So if Edna said things looked grim, they probably did. Alyce might need to leave for more reasons than one. Sharing a bedroom was minor. Breaking up her parents' marriage was major! If things kept up this way, she might have to find two husbands: one for Alyce and another for her mother!

A tear came into Angel's eye at the thought of losing Rudy. Rudy was the best thing that had ever happened to the family. Would he leave them all? Angel had trusted Rudy! But Alyce's presence might be just too much for any man.

Angel could see the handwriting on the wall, as her grandma always said when something was obvious. She didn't want to ignore the signs and be in what Edna called denial.

"Hey," said Edna, snapping her fingers. "Let's get to work here."

Angel was a million miles away, in an orphanage with Thena and Rags. Her mother was out working, and they had to sell the house to pay the bills. Rudy and Janet were together, living in Alyce's apartment near the office.

Edna snapped her fingers again. "Hey, reality check!" she said. "We're on planet Earth, here! I brought the ads." Edna unfolded a newspaper that she had under her arm. She spread it on the picnic table. She put the jug of lemonade on top of it to keep it from blowing away in the breeze.

Angel followed Edna's finger as it moved down the column.

"What's SWM?" she asked.

"Single white male," said Edna. "Just look at all we have to choose from! Mr. Right is somewhere in this paper, I'll bet you anything!"

"All these men want a wife?" shrieked Angel.

Edna nodded. "There are a lot of lonely guys out there."

"There are more than we need!" said Angel. "We're going to have men left over!"

Edna shook her head. "It isn't that easy," she said. "Some are too young. Some are real old guys. How old is Alyce?"

"Older than my mom," she said. "My mom is thirty-five."

"So Alyce is about forty?" asked Edna. "She looks older than that. Maybe she dyes her hair and she's really fifty."

"Then she might like a younger man with more pep," said Angel. "Then if they had a house he could shovel the sidewalk and cut the grass."

"That's true," said Edna. "And men die sooner than women, so young is good. Now we have to think of interests."

"Here is one who says he likes pets!" said Angel. "He has a pet boa constrictor."

Edna frowned. "That's a little bit extreme. Although I can see Alyce with a snake. She likes unusual things."

"I'll write his number down. It's 361J," said Angel.

"Here is a good one!" said Edna. "This guy has a boat and likes to go for midnight walks."

Angel shook her head. "Alyce gets carsick, so she probably gets seasick too. Anyway, she doesn't stay up that late; she's an early riser.

She tells me that all the time. 'Early to bed and early to rise makes a man healthy, wealthy, and wise.'"

"It didn't make her wealthy." Edna laughed. "Or even wise. Cross that guy off. He's too old, anyway. It says he's fifty-six."

"Here is a guy who speaks Chinese," said Angel. "Not many people can do that."

"That's not such a big deal," said Edna. "Here, I found another good one! 'Loves animals, gardening, and psychology. Tall, dark, and handsome, need someone to be my soul mate.' Doesn't that sound great? Alyce is always claiming she has ESP and can tell what people are thinking."

Angel wrote the number down. "Alyce is really lucky we're doing this. These guys are a great find. Do you think this is enough?"

"We've only got the pet snake and the ESP guy. Let's find one more so she has some choice."

The girls read up one column and down

another. Some men were too old, some too young, some liked to smoke (Alyce hated cigarettes and cigars), and some drank wine by the fire. (Alyce didn't believe in drinking wine.) (And Angel didn't think Alyce should meet anyone who liked fires.)

"I've got the last one!" said Edna, standing up. She wrote down the number 598C and folded the paper. "He's an orthodontist, and he eats health food," she said. "Isn't that wild? Alyce loves health food. Isn't she always mixing those drinks with alfalfa sprouts and garlic and soy milk?"

Angel made a face and nodded. "It's perfect. And he can fix her teeth if any get loose."

"Our job is almost done," said Edna. "One of these guys is the one who will take Alyce right out of your house for good. I only hope it's love at first sight."

"But how do we get Alyce to write to them?" Angel asked. "She might think she doesn't want to get married."

"She doesn't write to them." Edna sighed. "We do. I brought paper along. We can do it right now."

Angel felt nervous. Too much was happening too fast. And it didn't feel totally honest. It reminded her of Alyce's own words from a play she'd seen: "Oh what a tangled web we weave, / when first we practise to deceive!" Wasn't this practicing to deceive?

But deceit wasn't bothering Edna. She took a piece of stationery from her pocket.

"Dear Mr. 598C, I am a SWF looking for a SWM to eat health food with. I have my own juicer and raise herbs to cook tofu with. I also am interested in teeth. Do you like pets? If you don't, I can get rid of all mine. Love, Alyce."

"But they won't know whom to call," said Angel.

"They'll call Alyce, of course," said Edna. "I'll give them your number."

Things were moving too fast. What if her mom answered the phone? What if Rags answered? Or come to think of it, what if Alyce answered?

"Now you write the one to the snake man," said Edna, handing Angel the paper and pencil.

Angel couldn't seem to move, let alone write.

"Come on," said Edna. "Let's get on with this."

"Dear Snake Man," Angel wrote, trying to pick up Edna's enthusiasm. "I have pets too, and I'm sure my canary will be your boa's good friend."

"Unless he eats him!" roared Edna. "Snakes eat birds, you know."

Angel crossed off *canary* and wrote, "I'm sure my sheepdog will like your snake. Pets are nice, and I am thinking about going to school to be a veteran."

Edna frowned. "Do you mean *veterinarian?* A veteran's an old guy who fought in the war."

"I always get them mixed up," said Angel, crossing off *veteran* and writing *veterinarian.*

"Is she really going to school?" asked Edna.

"I didn't say she was *going* to school. I said she was thinking about it. I'm sure she has thought about it sometime in her life."

"Now the tall, dark, handsome guy with ESP," said Edna. "Dear Tall, Dark, and Handsome, I am tall, dark, and handsome too. Or you could call it pretty. I can read minds, like at parties, because I have ESP and I like gardens too, so we would have a lot of fun, especially if we got a house to live in out of town somewhere. Love, Alyce.

"I put that in about the house out of town so we could get things moving faster. No sense beating around the bush."

The girls put the letters in the envelopes, addressed them, and then walked to the post office to buy stamps. Edna put them in the slot and said, "This time tomorrow, Alyce will have herself a ticket out of your house."

Angel felt a shiver go down her spine. She crossed her fingers and even said a little prayer that Edna was right. *Please,* she prayed, *send the man with the ticket as soon as you can! And let Alyce fall in love with him at the first phone call.*

But Angel could not imagine how that could happen.

41

SIX

Mr. Wrong

The next morning, Angel's mother looked tired, even though she had just been out of bed for only a short time. *Maybe she is getting sick,* thought Angel. *Maybe she found out Rudy went to the park with Janet!* Angel looked so worried that her mom noticed.

"I'm fine," she said when Angel asked. "It's just this heat. The heat always bothers me."

But the heat never bothered her mom. She had loved the heat in Greece!

"And I guess Alyce's snoring did keep me awake last night," she added.

It had kept Angel awake too. Alyce was right in the bed next to her! But she didn't want to mention it and worry her mom even more. Angel wondered if she and Edna should be doing something even more drastic to get Alyce out, before she ruined the whole family. But what was more drastic than marriage?

Angel gave her mom a hug and said she and Edna would take Thena and Rags for a walk to the park. Her mother looked grateful. "Thank you, Caroline," she said.

The girls were gone for over an hour, and when they got back, Edna said, "Now Alyce will have talked to Mr. Right."

But inside was a note from Alyce saying that she had gone to the mall to look for curtains. And Angel's mom was taking a nap.

"I hope she's not getting curtains for my room!" said Angel. "I love my new curtains!"

That evening Angel asked Alyce if there had been any phone calls.

Alyce shook her head and looked puzzled. "Are you expecting someone to call you?" she asked.

"No," said Angel. "I'm not expecting anyone to call . . . *me*."

The next morning the phone rang very early. Mrs. Poppadopolis was giving Thena a bath. By the time Angel got to the phone, Alyce was just hanging it up.

"Some man asked for Ellis," she said. "It was the wrong number."

Angel had the nervous feeling that Ellis was Alyce and that Mr. Right was gone for good. Alyce's ticket out of town was canceled!

Angel got dressed and ran over to Edna's to tell her about the mistake. When they got back, Alyce said, "Another man called. Before I could ask what he wanted, he said he plans to be an animal doctor and help homeless dogs and cats!"

"Are you going to meet him?" shrieked Angel.

"Did you set up a date?" asked Edna.

"Now why would I do that?" asked Alyce. "It must have been a prank phone call. I'll tell your mother she should call the phone company and report it. Two strange phone calls in one day!"

Edna groaned. Angel wanted to tell Alyce about what they'd done, but she didn't think Alyce would like the idea of the girls looking for a husband for her without telling her. She might even think it was dishonest. It certainly did not feel like as good an idea as it had at first.

When Alyce left the room, Edna said, "If Alyce is going to hang up on these guys, our plan won't work. We have to hang around and answer the next one. There's only one call left!"

The girls played Parcheesi while they waited.

They read a book to Thena.

They read books to each other.

"Why aren't you girls outside, playing?" asked Angel's mother.

"It's too cold," said Angel.

"I think it's too warm," said Edna.

Mrs. Poppadopolis looked puzzled. When she took Athena out for a walk, the girls relaxed. Alyce was in the back yard mixing fertilizer for the floribunda. "Now!" said Edna. "If only he calls now, it will be a done deal!"

The girls crossed their fingers, but the phone did not ring.

"Maybe he's on vacation," said Angel.

"Or at work," said Edna.

Then, just as Rags rushed in the back door with Snowball, Alyce's cat, the phone rang. Rags picked it up and said, "Hello? No, Alyce isn't here." He hung up.

"Yes, she *is!*" screamed the girls, grabbing the phone. But it was too late. The third Mr. Right was gone.

Edna fell onto Angel's sofa and groaned.

"That was a guy we found to marry Alyce," said Edna to Rags. "And you ruined it."

"Where did you find him?" demanded Rags.

"In the paper," said Angel.

"That is dumb," said Rags, shaking his head. "That is so dumb."

If Rags thought the idea was dumb, thought Angel, it must really be dumb! What was Edna

thinking of? Even Rags could see she would not marry someone she never met! She wouldn't even talk to him! They were the wrong men. And Edna's idea was definitely the wrong idea!

What in the world could they do now?

SEVEN

Option Two

"What do we do now?" demanded Angel. In a way she was relieved that this idea was over, even though they did not have any new idea to replace it.

"We go on to option two," said Edna. "The blind date. We fix her up ourselves with someone we handpick."

"Handpicked" was what a sign said in the market her mom went to for fruit. It sounded as if Edna was going to pick a man off a tree, like an apple.

Well, at least a real man was better than a man from a newspaper. Angel wondered where they would handpick him.

As she wondered, Bubba rushed in the door and shook muddy water and fertilizer from his heavy coat all over the girls, the furniture, and the walls.

"Yikes!" shouted Angel.

"I say we get busy on plan two right now," said Edna.

"Plan two?" said Alyce, coming in behind Bubba. She had as much fertilizer on her as Bubba did.

Angel brought in a towel, and said "Plan to go on vacation."

Alyce laughed. "You are just back from vacation!" she said.

"Plan two for a hus—" Rags began and Angel put her hand over his mouth.

"For a house," said Angel. "That's what he meant, a house...cleaning! This house needs to be cleaned!"

The girls said good-bye and left Alyce looking puzzled.

"We should not tell Rags anything!" said Edna when they got outside. "He is a trouble-maker! He's going to mess up our plan."

Angel wasn't sure it was Rags this time. *He* knew the idea was a dumb one. Why didn't they?

But they did have to try something. Angel's whole sweet bedroom was probably full of mud by now. Bubba had to go. And that meant Alyce had to go. And all of her belongings. And the only hope Angel had of getting rid of her were the ideas in Edna's head.

"What about the blind date?" asked Angel.

"A blind date means we find Mr. Right our-selves," said Edna. "We go up to a guy we know, like Mr. Foggs, the butcher, and say, 'Would you like to go to a movie with Alyce tonight?'"

"Alyce goes to her exercise class tonight," said Angel, frowning.

"Well, tomorrow night then!" said Edna.

"The night is not the point! The point is we find someone and introduce them!"

"Alyce doesn't eat meat. I don't think she would be happy with a man who cut up meat for a living."

"That was just an example. We could choose, say, the postman, Mr. Glaser, who delivers the mail."

Angel frowned and shook her head. "And what about Mrs. Glaser?" she asked.

"All right, a bad idea. Have you got a better one?" asked Edna.

Angel thought. "Maybe we just need a roommate for her," she said. "Like Janet, the clown Rudy works with."

Edna shook her head. "Alyce would choose your house over an apartment with Janet. Janet isn't rich or romantic, and Alyce needs a family. Kids. No, a roommate is no good."

The girls lay back on the grass to think. Angel wanted to fall asleep and wake up when Alyce was gone. But she knew it wasn't that easy. This was going to take work.

There was music coming from the house, from Angel's bedroom window, to be exact. Alyce was using Angel's CD player. It was a song with Italian words in it.

"Alyce is taking Italian lessons," said Angel. "She says next summer all of us can go to Italy together."

"Scary," said Edna.

Then both girls jumped, because they heard Angel's mother's voice.

"Where did you ever come up with such a silly idea?"

Her voice sounded cross. She must have been talking to Rags. But it was not Rags that answered her. It was Rudy's voice that responded.

"You act like this isn't my house too," he said.

Edna whistled through her teeth. "Looks like trouble," she said. "Your mom sounds mad at Rudy. I hope it isn't *him* who moves out instead of Alyce."

While the girls were wondering what to do, a man with a mustache and a small beard and carrying a suitcase got out of a car and came over to them. On the side of the car it read, "Waterless Cookware." In smaller letters it said "Ten-year guarantee! Invite me in to cook for you."

"Are you girls hungry by any chance?" he called to them. "I have this bag of food to demonstrate my cookware, and my last appointment canceled on me. I'd hate my beef to spoil. I make a mean stroganoff your family would love."

The man sat down on the grass on the other side of Angel's fence and said, "My name is Clifford, and I hope you have a family in that big house that you'd like dinner for."

He smiled and seemed friendly. But he *was* a stranger. Angel had to be cautious, even though she was very hungry because of Alyce's burned offerings at lunchtime.

Edna did not worry about strangers. She took one look at the man's handsome face and bag of food and jumped up, reached her hand over

the fence, and said, "Hi, I'm Edna, and we do have a big family. Are you married?"

The man laughed. "No, but I think I'm a little old for you!"

"Get your pots," said Edna. "And come in. I'll set the table."

EIGHT

Dinner for Eight
(or Four or Six)

Edna reached into Angel's cupboard and took out eight plates. "I'll call my mom and ask if I can stay too," she said to Angel. "I think it's what my dad would call a business dinner."

It was quiet in the house. After the argument, everyone seemed to have left. Even the Italian music had stopped. Angel wondered if she should let a stranger cook dinner without asking her mom. It felt like something you should get permission for. Things were so mixed up lately that Angel wasn't sure if the old rules still held. But a dinner already cooked would be one less thing for her mother to worry about. She had a lot on her mind.

"It will be a surprise for them when they come home. Where do you keep your napkins?" asked Edna.

Just then Angel's mother came down the stairs with baby Thena. Her eyes were red as if she may have been crying, but maybe she was just sunburned from working in the garden, thought Angel.

"Mom, this is Clifford. He wants to cook dinner for us and demonstrate his cookware. His last appointment canceled and his beef might spoil."

Clifford reached out his hand and shook the hand of Mrs. Poppadopolis. He handed her his card and a brochure about his cookware.

"Why, how nice," said Mrs. Poppadopolis. "That would be a nice change from ... our regular cooking! But in ten minutes I have to be at the nursing home to help with the birthday party of the month."

"I'll save you a plate of stroganoff," said Clifford. If he was disappointed to lose a customer, he didn't say so. He did point out the fine points of his product to Angel's mother while she was getting ready to leave. Thena seemed to be listening too.

"You'll be able to tell how well it works when you taste the food tonight," he said. He handed Thena a spoon to play with. "These pans enhance the flavors, and the food retains all the vitamins."

Mrs. Poppadopolis promised to study the brochure that evening.

"I'm taking Thena with me," said Angel's mom. "The people in the home love to see her." Angel knew something was very wrong—her mother was leaving her at home with a stranger who was cooking in their kitchen!

Thena waved bye-bye.

Edna took two plates off the table.

Clifford looked over the kitchen work area and went to the car to get the rest of his supplies.

"I have all my own equipment," he said.

One by one he brought in boxes. Some had food in them. Some had the cookware, all shiny and clean. And some had gadgets like potato peelers and mashers.

"Would you like to peel carrots?" he asked the girls politely.

The girls pitched in and peeled. Clifford put his cookware on the stove and said he hoped the girls would like the dinner and tell their relatives about it.

"You will see at dinnertime!" he said, browning thin strips of beef in a little oil. He put some spices on them, and they sizzled away and filled the whole kitchen with delicious smells. Angel's mouth was watering. Noodles were bubbling away in another pan. Although Clifford said the cookware was waterless, it looked to Angel like it was water the noodles were boiling in.

"Alyce will buy some, I'm sure," said Edna to Clifford. "She's a friend of the family. She will be getting married soon, and she loves to cook."

"And who is this lucky man she will marry?"

asked Clifford as he mixed low-fat sour cream in a small bowl.

Angel hoped Edna did not shout out *"You!"* and scare Clifford to death.

"We aren't exactly sure yet," said Edna. "But she wants to marry very badly."

The smells brought Rags down into the kitchen. He did not seem surprised to see a stranger cooking dinner.

"When can we eat?" he shouted. "Can I have seconds?"

Clifford explained the theory behind waterless cookware to Rags. Rags nibbled on a carrot and nodded when Clifford told him what miracles happened with his pots and pans.

"What smells so good?" asked Rudy, coming into the room rubbing his hands together. Clifford reached out to shake his hand and told Rudy about his cookware and the beef stroganoff he was making for dinner.

"What a lucky thing you came by," said Rudy. "The kids can use a good dinner! Wish I could be here, but Janet and I have to do a show at the Children's Hospital. I wonder if you could keep a plate hot for me?"

"You bet I can!" said Clifford. "You wouldn't want to miss this meal!"

"Do you want to come along to the show, Rags?" asked his dad.

Rags was torn between the show and the stroganoff.

"I'll save you both a big plate of food!" said Clifford, draining his noodles.

"Great!" said Rags, running to get washed up.

Rudy gave Angel and Edna a hug and told them to hold down the fort while he got his costume ready for the show.

Edna took two more plates off the table.

"I guess there's only four of us now," said Edna, washing some mushrooms the way Clifford showed her.

Clifford snapped his fingers and ran out to the car for his serving dish. When he came back, there was a boy with him about Angel's age. He looked a lot like Clifford, only sleepier.

"This is my son Fendell," smiled Clifford. "He was taking a nap in the back seat. In the summer I take my boy along on the road with me."

The girls said hello to Fendell. Fendell shook their hands and yawned. "Pleased to meet you all," he said.

Edna rolled her eyes at Angel.

"I thought he said he wasn't married," whispered Angel to Edna. "Where there is a son there is a wife!"

"He must be divorced," said Edna frowning. "I'm not sure Alyce is ready for motherhood. I know I'd hate to have her for a mother."

A son was going to complicate things, that was for sure, thought Angel. If Alyce liked privacy, there wouldn't be much. Fendell would be there.

"We never agreed on a son," grumbled Edna, slicing the mushrooms. "Now Alyce won't even be interested in him in a romantic way. She'll think he's married!"

Edna put another plate on the table for

Fendell. "Things are not going well," she said.

Just then Alyce burst in the back door. A short man with kind blue eyes followed her. Bubba nipped at his heels. Bubba sniffed the air and put his front feet on Clifford's shoulders.

"Whoa, down boy!" said Clifford, juggling a bowl of noodles.

"This is Rocco," said Alyce. "We're on our way to go bowling, but I thought I'd get dinner for my little darlings first."

Alyce sniffed the air. Then she noticed Clifford.

"This is Alyce," said Edna to Clifford.

Clifford reached out his hand again.

"So you are the bride to be!" said Clifford. "And this must be the lucky groom! Well, you don't have to worry about dinner tonight! Why don't you join us before you leave? Everything is ready. Chow's on!"

Edna got another plate and put it on the table.

NINE

Plates On, Plates Off

"We'll be having a pretzel at the alley," said Alyce, looking at her watch. "I'm just glad these darling children will have dinner. I've been doing the cooking, and I don't mind saying it will be good to have a little break."

Edna took two plates off the table.

It appeared that Alyce had heard only the last thing Clifford said, about staying for dinner. Rocco was listening to Clifford's sales pitch now and nodding his head.

"You'll be needing a set like this, being married and all," Clifford concluded.

Rocco shook his head. "My wife doesn't like to cook," he said.

Clifford looked confused.

Edna looked distressed. Although most of her plans went well, this one was a disaster.

Angel was much more worried about her mother and Rudy than she was about Alyce's love life. And yet, if Alyce's love life did not go well, she might never leave, and that meant Rudy would find Janet more and more attractive!

Angel wondered if other girls her age had problems that weighed this heavily on their shoulders. The ones she knew at school seemed to worry about makeup and hairstyles and new bikes. Angel never seemed to have time to think about things like that. It seemed from the time she'd been small, or at any rate, since Rags was born, the family problems were her problems. Rudy had been a godsend, but now even this looked like it was in jeopardy.

The current problem could be said in one word: Alyce! Alyce was trouble no matter where she was, but especially when she was in their big green house. Of course no man could marry her! They would go crazy with the cat hair and garden mud and fires and burned food. And she did not seem to hear what people said lately. Maybe she was getting hard of hearing and needed a hearing aid.

"There's a man for every woman," Angel's grandma used to say. Well, if this was true, where in the world was the one for Alyce? In another city, another country, another planet?

Alyce and Rocco now left, and Fendell said, "Does he have any toys?"

At first Angel thought he meant Rocco! This whole thing was too confusing for words!

"The dog," said Fendell. "I thought we could play fetch."

Bubba heard the word *fetch* and ran to get his red rubber ring.

"That's it, boy!" said Fendell, patting him on the head. "What a smart dog," he added.

"Soup's on!" said Clifford. "Wash up!"

The girls went upstairs to wash their hands, and Fendell washed up at the kitchen sink.

"I can't believe we have a perfectly good husband right here, and Alyce walks out with some other guy who's married!" said Edna. "Why is she going out with a married guy, anyway?"

"They are on the same bowling team," said Angel.

"Well, it looks fishy to me," said Edna. "Like Rudy and Janet. Nothing good can come of it."

Clifford's dinner was very good. After he served the four of them, he filled the other plates, covered them, and put them in the oven on "warm."

"This will taste pretty good when they come home tired and hungry!" said Clifford.

It tasted pretty good to Angel right then. She finished the buttery noodles and beef strips and asked for more. So did Edna and Fendell.

"It's all because of the cookware!" said Clifford. "Mouthwatering, is what it is. And packed with vitamins."

Angel didn't care about the vitamins or the pots and pans it had cooked in. She just cared that she was finally having a good dinner — the first since Alyce had moved back in.

Angel noticed that Fendell had very good table manners. He didn't put his elbows on the table or make mouth noises like Rags, and he asked politely when he wanted the bread passed, or the salt and pepper. Perhaps Fendell ate dinner with the families that his father cooked for all the time! Angel thought it might be a good idea if you could order good manners for your family at the same time you bought cookware. It might be something that Edna could work on. A free course in table manners with every set of pots and pans sold! Maybe a coupon could be enclosed. She'd tell Edna about the idea.

Or maybe it was another idea that her wild imagination had come up with. She wished she could tell the difference between a good idea and a wild one before she acted on it. It could avoid a lot of trouble.

When they were almost through with dinner, the phone rang. Angel answered it. It was Alyce's landlord.

"I'm sorry to report the damage is worse than it appeared," he said. "It's going to take longer than we thought for repairs. We just can't say when this place will be livable. But we'll give her a call when she can move back in. Could you give Alyce that message?"

Angel's spirits fell. Even the good dinner could not offset this news. Alyce would be here forever. Angel knew it. The apartment would never be fixed. The landlord would never want her and her animals and fire hazards back. School would start and she would be here. It would end in spring and she would be here. When Angel graduated from college Alyce would be here. She and Alyce would grow old together and have white hair like her grandma and false teeth and canes, and when Alyce got down to weed the garden she would not be able to get up. They would eat meals on wheels with

Rudy and her mom—Rags and Thena would be off married and living in another state and having children of their own. Angel could see all this in her mind's eye as clearly as if it were happening then.

"I'll tell her," said Angel and hung up. Her eyelid began to twitch.

She and Edna had to double their attempts to find Alyce a husband.

There was no time to lose.

TEN

Fendell Finds a Way

When the family came home and ate Clifford's dinner, Rudy rubbed his stomach and said, "I'll take a set of this cookware, Cliff. Maybe I'll learn to make this stroganoff myself!" He winked at his wife.

Angel gave Alyce the phone message, and she frowned. "With my cousins coming for a visit, I was hoping I'd have my own place again! I'll just have to make do, I guess. We'll just hang 'em from the rafters right here!"

"Hang 'em from the rafters! Cafters, bafters, rafters!" sang Rags.

74

Angel thought her mother turned a bit pale at those words, and she didn't praise Rags for his rhyme. Instead she said, "Hush, Rags." Rags looked like he might pout.

Angel couldn't wait to meet with Edna alone. What they had on their hands was a crisis. They needed a crisis specialist. She was beginning to think this was more than they could handle alone.

Fendell had brought in his Clue game from the car, and he, Angel, Edna, and Rags played a game. But Angel couldn't keep her mind on it and lost.

By morning, word had got around town that Clifford was a good cook, and quite a few people asked him to do a demonstration in their home.

"I think we'll be in Elm City for a long time," he said. "Thanks for giving me a chance. No matter how many houses I cook in, I'll always think of this house as home!"

"And you should!" cooed Alyce. "In fact, perhaps if we all squeeze a bit, you can stay here with us. It's always nice to bunk with friends instead of strangers."

Angel couldn't believe her ears! It wasn't even Alyce's house, and she was inviting yet more people to live with them. The last thing they needed now, thought Angel, was another person to call her big green house home. Actually, it wasn't so crowded. It just looked that way because Alyce always seemed like a crowd instead of just one person.

Rudy held up his hand. "I think this hotel is filled!" He laughed.

"I've already signed us up at the Elm City Motel," said Clifford. "They have good beds and a little kitchenette for us to cook our own breakfast."

"Hey, Fendell can come over and play Clue with us every day now!" said Rags.

"I'll bring my action figures tomorrow," said Fendell.

Edna rolled her eyes and Angel groaned. Even if Clifford and Fendell did not move in, they were here a lot. Clifford was becoming a friend of Rudy's. The night before, they had played cribbage together. Between Janet and Clifford and Fendell and Alyce's relatives, her parents definitely would be without privacy, thought Angel. Their marriage was a disaster waiting to happen.

The next morning Angel and Edna sat in the park with their notebooks.

"I think the problem is too big to handle ourselves," said Angel. "We need professional help."

"Help for what?" said a voice behind them. It was Fendell.

Both Angel and Edna started talking at once. They told him the problem with Alyce and said that the best solution would be if his dad would marry her.

Fendell shook his head. "I don't think that's the answer," he said. "When my parents had problems they went to a counselor. That really helped. They got a divorce."

"A counselor is supposed to *save* a marriage," said Angel.

"We'll never get your parents to a shrink," said

Edna. "That's a marriage counselor," she added. "She would just say to get rid of Alyce, anyway."

"What you need is a counselor for Alyce," said Fendell. "When she goes, everything will be normal again."

"We'd never get her to go to one," said Edna.

"A counselor would tell Alyce to be independent," said Fendell. "To get out of your house and get a job and get a life."

The girls stared at Fendell. He knew a lot.

"I had to go to therapy with my parents," he said. "I learned lots of stuff about grownups. They really can get messed up. They need kids to straighten them out sometimes."

"Well, we know she should move out," said Edna. "We just have to find a way to do it."

"If she got a job, she'd have money to rent a new apartment, and she wouldn't need a husband," said Fendell. "Counselors don't advise dependency. Alyce shouldn't look for someone else to lean on."

Edna leaped to her feet. "That's it!" she said.

"Instead of a husband, we get her a job! That's much more cool anyway!"

The girls stared at Fendell with new respect. It was a good omen that had sent Clifford and his waterless cookware to their door. Fendell was smart. He had been to counseling. He understood the problem. He was heaven-sent!

"Let's make an agenda," said Fendell, taking a small notebook out of his pocket. It had a tiny pencil attached. The notebook was one more sign that Fendell was a soul mate — he was smart and creative and had an imagination.

At the top of the first page, Fendell wrote, "Goal." "It's important to set goals," he said. "We have to know the direction we are going in."

Angel thought Edna was smart, but she never had been in real, honest-to-goodness counseling. No, Fendell was definitely a step up on the ladder of problem solving.

"I think we all know our goal," he said. "Independence and self-sufficiency for Alyce." He wrote that down as the girls watched him. It looked to Angel like all the words were spelled right.

"Now," he went on. "The next thing is how we attain this goal. What means do we use to obtain that independence."

Where had this boy come from? No wonder his father could sell cookware! He should probably be a rocket scientist! This was a family of goal setters! Angel didn't know many boys, except the ones in her class. Well, and Rags of course, but he was too undeveloped to count. And Rudy was too overdeveloped to count. But Fendell seemed like just the kind of boy who would grow up to be a hard worker. Even president. The kind of boy who would grow up to be someone Angel would consider... marrying!

The word scared her! What if she should fall in love? What if she turned boy crazy like some of the girls in her class? She would have to be careful. She had no room in her life for another worry. Especially one of this size.

Edna was jumping up and down. "A *job!* Write it down!"

Fendell wrote it down. "Means: A job for Alyce."

How easy! How clear! Their problem was solved!

But it wasn't long before Angel realized that *thinking* of a job was not the same as *getting* a job.

"Number three," wrote Fendell. "Method of obtaining a job for Alyce."

Under this he wrote "1, 2," and "3."

"Where do we find her a job?" asked Angel.

"The want ads," said Edna.

Angel did not have a good feeling about want ads. So far, they had led nowhere.

Fendell held up his hand. "What does she like to do, is the first thing to ask. We want to place her in the right profession, so that she will enjoy it and do a good job and not get fired."

Fired. Angel did not like that word. It sounded like something that could definitely happen to Alyce. Even once they got her a job, she might get fired!

Problems were piling up. But then no one ever said life would be easy. That is what her grandma in Saint Paul often reminded her. And as usual, she was right.

ELEVEN

A Brand-New Problem

"What are her interests?" repeated Fendell. "What does she like to do?"

"Well, scratch cooking," Edna frowned. "Anything to do with fire is out."

"She could use a microwave," said Angel.

"Even without fire, she is no great shakes with food," said Edna.

"What about horticulture?" asked Fendell. "I noticed she was weeding the other day."

"She knows the difference between plants and weeds," said Angel, wishing she had her dictionary nearby. She would have to get one of those pocket-size dictionaries to carry with her.

Fendell wrote down "nursery."

Angel shook her head. "She is a bit forgetful with babies," she said. "I wouldn't trust her in a nursery."

Edna rolled her eyes. She and Fendell smiled. "A nursery is where they raise plants to sell," said Fendell.

They were laughing at her, thought Angel. Three was not a good number for friendship. Rudy had told her that. Angel felt left out already. Her best friend and Fendell knew something she didn't!

"Does she have a good bedside manner?" asked Fendell. He seemed to be talking only to Edna. This was *Angel's* problem. Edna hardly knew Alyce!

Edna shook her head. "If she were a nurse, she'd forget to give people their medicine on time."

"Well, she'd need a degree for that profession,

anyway," said Fendell. "But she could be a medical aid, work in a nursing home," Fendell went on.

"I don't think so," said Angel. "She is too absent-minded."

"I think she'd be good with old people," said Edna.

Fendell wrote down, "nursing home assistant."

Angel's eye was beginning to twitch.

Now Fendell and Edna moved to another park bench and discussed other things Alyce could do and be, without consulting Angel at all. Edna seemed to giggle a lot. She tossed her hair over her shoulder and twisted one loop around her finger. She was flirting with Fendell! Edna was boy crazy! Her best friend was trying to take this boy away for herself! Pretty soon she and Fendell would be dating and going to movies, and Angel would be back in the yard with Rags, friendless and lonely and eating Alyce's burned food for the rest of her life!

First it was Alyce moving in.

Then it was Rudy fighting with her mom.

Then it was Rudy running off with Janet.

And now it looked as if she would lose her best friend to the waterless cookware salesman's son. What else could go wrong?

All right, let them flirt. Let them run off and leave her behind. But she didn't have to sit here and watch. She would go home to her green house and her little blue and white room.

But when she got there, she remembered it wasn't her room anymore. It was Alyce's. Maybe she should leave home, run away, take a train out of town, fly to Australia.

But whom did she know in Australia? And everything was upside down there. Summer was in winter and winter was in summer. Angel had enough problems without adding that kind of confusion. She didn't want to travel alone, and now she had no best friend to go with her. She had wanted to come home from Greece, where people loved her. Surely she would not like Australia, where people didn't. She threw herself onto Alyce's beanbag chair beside Snowball and cried. Snowball curled up closer to her and purred, but this did not make Angel feel better.

In a little while Angel heard a door slam. She heard footsteps running up the stairs. Her door opened and Edna burst in.

"What's the matter with you?" shouted Edna crossly. "Why did you run away?"

Edna had her hands on her hips. "We're trying to help *you*, for heaven's sake!"

Edna acted as if Angel had dreamed Edna had been flirting with Fendell. She acted like she had not been keeping Fendell to herself and leaving her out. She was acting like Angel was crazy to be upset about it. She acted like Angel's imagination had gone wild again.

Had it? Angel didn't think so. She knew what she saw. She knew what she knew. Edna was in love with Fendell. And they didn't want Angel around.

"Come on!" said Edna, giving Angel a pull on her sleeve. "We have work to do. Fendell had to go help his dad shop."

Oh, fine. Now Angel was good enough, when Fendell was gone. But he would be back, and then Angel would be dumped again. And hurt again. Life was so cruel. At this rate Angel would never live long enough to grow old with Alyce!

"Come on," said Edna again, more gently. "Fendell made some suggestions for our next move. He's really good at problem solving."

Angel got up, wiped her eyes, and followed Edna downstairs.

"I made you some tuna sandwiches for lunch," said Angel's mother. "Maybe you and Edna would like to eat them out in the back yard at the picnic table. Will Fendell be joining you?"

Edna shook her head. "He's gone shopping with his dad," she said.

Rags bounced into the kitchen, looking for lunch.

"Look!" he said, holding up his hands. Each fingernail was painted a different color. Blue, red, yellow, green, gold. "Alyce did it!" he said.

Alyce came into the room holding Thena. As Thena waved her little hands, Angel could see that she had brightly colored fingernails too. And, glancing at Thena's bare feet, the girls noticed her toenails were the same.

"Alyce has too much time on her hands," Edna whispered to Angel.

The girls took their lunch outside in the shade, and Edna pulled out Fendell's list.

For a moment, Angel forgot her jealousy problem. There was work to do, before she and Edna ended up with their fingernails and toenails painted all colors of the rainbow too!

TWELVE

Empowering Alyce

"Fendell had this brainstorm," said Edna, chewing her tuna sandwich. "He left me in charge of carrying it off while he is gone."

Angel rolled her eyes. So who died and made Edna queen? Why in the world did Fendell think he could put Edna in charge? *Well,* thought Angel, answering her question, *because no one stopped him!*

"Here it is," said Edna. "He says first of all we have to get her used to the idea of working. We have to sort of set the stage. If we get her a job, she won't take it if she is not prepared. They call this *mo-tiv-a-tion*."

Edna talked to Angel as if she were a child, a very young child. She pronounced *motivation* with four distinct parts.

"Don't talk like a teacher," said Angel.

Edna rolled her eyes. "Fendell says it's up to the three of us to let her know how much a job would ben-e-fit her. How in-de-pen-dent she can become! He says that is called em-pow-er-ing women."

Maybe Fendell was older than they were. A lot older.

"She is-not-going-to-buy-that," said Angel, acting like a teacher herself.

"This is not going to be easy if you have that negative attitude," said Edna.

The girls looked at Alyce making sandcastles in the sandbox with Thena and Rags. Angel followed Edna over to them.

Thena was jumping up and down in excitement. She had sand in her hair and on her sun suit.

"See the castle!" said Alyce, who was adding some water to make the sand stick together. Rags was filling his shoes with wet sand and making molded feet.

"It's a long, long day, isn't it?" said Edna yawning. "I wish we had a job to go to, some way to earn money. More people should have jobs and become productive citizens."

"Why, my dog groomer needs people to pick berries on her farm," said Alyce, looking interested. "You girls could do that! It would keep you busy and earn you a little money! Why don't I give her a call?"

Alyce began to brush sand from her pants and start toward the house.

Edna ran after her. "No, we don't want to pick berries!" she called.

"What's the matter with berry picking?" asked Alyce. "It's fine, honest work."

While Edna was thinking of what to say, Alyce went on. "Well, Rocco needs young people to hand out fliers to the houses in town advertising his business. That would be outdoors too,

in the healthy summer air. Let me give Rocco a call. I can set you girls up with that job in no time flat."

Edna held up her hand. "Alyce, we can't take a job now; school is going to start in a couple of weeks."

"These jobs would only last a week," said Alyce. "I'll be glad to put in a good word for you."

Edna walked away, and Angel followed her.

"Geez Louise," said Edna. "That sure backfired!"

"Maybe Fendell wants to pick berries or deliver fliers," said Angel, smiling. Even though she wanted Alyce to get a job, she liked the fact that Edna wasn't doing a great job of being in charge.

"You're missing the whole point," said Edna, stamping her foot. "We are trying to get *Alyce* a job, not the other way around!"

Soon Fendell came by, and he frowned when he heard the story. They played a game of Clue with Rags while they thought about their problem, and before long Alyce came out and invited Edna and Fendell to stay for supper.

"I'm making my famous crab cakes," she said. "Tender and moist. I don't have any crab, but I'm using anchovies instead. That should make them even better. A fish is a fish, I always say!"

"I hate anchovies!" said Edna after Alyce had gone back into the house. "But I feel it is my job to stay and use this chance to empower Alyce."

"And get her a job that isn't in the kitchen," said Fendell.

He laughed at his own joke, and Edna laughed even harder, as if he had said something funnier than the comedians on TV.

"Get her out of the kitchen. That's really funny!" cried Edna, slapping her sides.

Angel didn't see anything funny about it. After all, Alyce tried to do a good job. She liked to cook and help out, and she liked to take care of her little adopted family. Didn't Edna and Fendell see that?

But at suppertime Angel remembered why Alyce did not belong in the kitchen. The crab cakes with anchovies were salty. Very, very salty. Everyone was drinking lots of water and milk and soda.

"Oh, girls," said Alyce. "I forgot to tell you, you can start picking berries in the morning! And if Fendell wants the delivery job, it's his!"

This was not going well. When would empowering Alyce (instead of them) begin?

Rudy said the crab cakes were good and asked for seconds. "Janet got a new job today," he said cheerfully. "At station KLOX."

Well, that was some help, thought Angel. With Janet out of the way, it would be easier to fix the troubled marriage.

"A new job, you say?" said Fendell. "I like to see women trying to improve themselves. More money, more independence!"

"Well, it's closer to her house," said Rudy.

"There are so many jobs in town!" said Edna. "Everyone needs help. It's a wonderful time to earn money to, say, buy a house of your own or rent a big apartment."

"My cousin just got a bigger apartment!" said Fendell. "He got a new job repairing computers."

"My aunt is selling Marry Faye face products," said Edna. "Door to door. She won the employee-of-the-month award, one hundred dollars! She's going to save up and buy a car so she can be really independent and not have to ask anyone for a ride."

"I say a woman's place is in the home," said Alyce, bringing in more anchovy cakes from the oven. They were not burned. They were raw in the middle.

"In the home!" shouted Edna. "That is really old-fashioned stuff."

"Well, I worked for a long time, and I like being home with my children," said Angel's mother. "Old-fashioned or not, Rudy takes good care of us."

Edna looked angry.

Angel hoped that her mother was right, and that Rudy would continue to take care of them. But if Alyce didn't get empowered soon, it might not happen!

THIRTEEN

Alyce the Hamburger

After supper everyone helped with the dishes, and then the girls went out on the porch.

"I think she's getting the idea," said Fendell. "Let's get the applications tomorrow."

In the morning Fendell and the girls trudged around Elm City asking for applications wherever they saw "Help Wanted" signs in the window.

"You must be sixteen or older," said one cross man in the drugstore.

"Oh, it's not for *us!*" said Edna. "It's for someone who is way more than sixteen! We are just helping her out."

But the man stomped off and did not reply.

At the landscape nursery the owner said, "The only help we need is people to prune trees."

"That's okay," said Angel. "Alyce can prune, can't she?" She turned to Edna and Fendell.

They both nodded. "Of course," they said. "She can prune." They took the application.

At the nursing home the director said they did not need any help.

"Our friend could take flowers to the rooms when someone sends them," said Fendell.

"Our volunteers do that," said the man. "Would your friend like to volunteer?"

"She can't work without pay!" said Edna. "How could she pay her rent? I'll bet you don't ask men to volunteer! You should help to empower women, sir. No offense, but you are behind the times."

The man smiled. He said, "Well, we could

use someone to mop the floors and change the beds."

"Fine," said Edna. "As long as it pays real money."

"I don't think mopping and changing beds is the same as working with old people," said Angel.

"There would be old people all around her," said Edna.

"Maybe these two are enough," said Fendell. "Let's fill them out."

"Isn't Alyce going to fill them out?" said Angel.

"Alyce doesn't know she wants a job," said Edna. "Filling out applications might scare her away. We'll just do it for her."

Edna and Fendell sat on the curb and put their heads together. They whispered and giggled as they filled in the spaces. Angel walked across the street to an empty lot and lay down in the grass. No one missed her.

For being so smart, Fendell was dumb, she thought. If filling out applications would scare

Alyce, why did he think she would actually take a job? She had to know about the job before she could go to work!

And couldn't Fendell see through Edna's flirting? Didn't he realize she was acting boy crazy? Unless boys liked boy-crazy girls. Maybe they did. Maybe they were all girl crazy!

Angel sighed and nodded off. How could she figure out life's problems if she didn't understand any of them? If they kept changing? People never acted the way they should. They were not sensible. Angel drifted off and dreamed that Alyce became her mother, and her mother became a nun in the convent behind Saint Mary's, and Rudy became a waterless cookware salesman, and Rags became president. When she woke up, Edna and Fendell were looking down at her.

"Wake up!" said Edna. "We're doing all the work! We have to drop these applications off where we got them. We've got them all filled out."

Maybe her friends, or former friends, knew something she didn't know, thought Angel. Maybe they knew how they would get Alyce off to work even if she didn't know she had a job.

But after the applications were returned, Fendell made the plan clear. "Before they hire her," he said, "we have to use subliminal persuasion to plant the idea of work in her head. It's real subtle. They use it to sell stuff, like hamburgers."

Angel did not think Alyce was in any way like a hamburger, but she didn't say anything.

"Putting the idea of a hamburger in someone's head is like putting the idea of work in your head. We just hang around Alyce and keep using the words *job* and *work* and *nurses* and *pruning* over and over till it gets in her head and she's just dying to go out to work. It's the latest thing. The power of suggestion, only it's unconscious," said Fendell.

"I know all about that," said Edna.

Edna was lying, thought Angel. Edna never

mentioned knowing about something called subliminal persuasion. She never used to lie, but now that she was boy crazy, she was changing. She wanted Fendell to like her, so she pretended.

"We have to start right now," said Fendell, "because the nursing home or the nursery might call soon. Both of them will want to hire her. We made her sound very suitable."

More lies, thought Angel. Well, perhaps she did know how to mop and change beds, and maybe she could prune. Maybe they are just white lies.

When they got close to Angel's house, Fendell said, "Look! We're lucky! Alyce is in the yard, weeding! We can practice our S.P.!"

The only S.P. Angel knew were salt and pepper. She frowned.

"That's the psychological jargon for subliminal persuasion," said Edna. "All the pros use it." She rolled her eyes at Fendell.

Fendell threw himself on the lawn beside Alyce. "That's quite a *job,* isn't it, Alyce?" he asked.

"Well I could use a little help," she said.

"Speaking of *help*, good *help* is hard to find," said Edna.

Edna jabbed Angel in the ribs; it was her turn to help out.

"I could *prune* those bushes for you," Angel said to Alyce.

"I'll do that later in the fall," said Alyce. "Fall is the time to prune, you know. Let's give it a couple of weeks."

A couple of weeks. A couple of months. A couple of years was more like it. Her statements brought to mind that Alyce would be around for a long, long time.

Rudy came out of the house on his way to the TV station. When he walked by, he said, "That's a lot of work, Alyce! Glad to see you're on the job!"

Now Rudy was doing it! S.P. was contagious!

"I'll bet someone with a great big garden would *hire* you, Alyce," said Fendell.

"No, no, no!" said Rudy, getting into his car. "She's doing a fine job right here. I'm not ready to fire her yet! We need good workers."

Well, thought Angel, *if Alyce isn't getting the message now, she never will.* There were surely enough job words used to sell a lot of hamburgers! But Fendell drummed on.

"I'll bet it really *pays* to keep those weeds out," he said.

Alyce wiped her forehead with a dirty glove and said, "Idle hands are the devil's workshop."

"Exactly!" said Edna. "That's what my mom always says! People should all be *employed* in meaningful *work!*"

"Work, work, work, there's lots of it around a house," said Alyce.

"And other places," said Angel, trying to do her part. "Like offices and nursing homes and nurseries."

"They need people to *mop* in nursing homes," said Edna. "And *prune* in nurseries. Pruning is really important."

"And fun!" said Fendell. "Wham, wham, off go those branches!"

"Prune, prune, prune," said Angel. "Especially in the fall."

Rags came down the steps with his coloring book and crayons. He lay down on the grass next to Alyce and began to color a picture of a lady selling rolls in a bakery.

"Look!" said Angel. "The woman in the picture is *working* in the bakery. Selling sweet rolls to a customer!" One picture is worth a thousand words, Angel's mother often told her. At that rate, the picture should get Alyce out working fast!

Rags colored the sweet roll brown. "That looks good enough to eat," said Alyce, tousling his hair. "You are a good little artist."

Alyce stood up and brushed herself off. "Well, that's it for today," she said.

"Are you going downtown?" asked Angel.

"Why would I go downtown now?"

"Do you have any special thing you feel like doing?" Edna asked Alyce.

"Urges?" asked Fendell.

Everyone waited and looked.

Alyce frowned. "I do," she said. "I have this overwhelming desire for — "

"Yes? Yes? What?" shouted Fendell and the girls.

"I seem to have the urge to eat a great big prune Danish!" she said.

FOURTEEN

One Crowded Bedroom

Alyce washed up, put Thena in the stroller, and set off for the bakery.

"Well, it did work," said Fendell grimly. "I mean the word *prune* and the picture of the sweet roll got through to her subliminally. It worked."

"If it worked, Alyce would be working right now," said Angel.

"Well, if you can do any better, go ahead," said Edna. "We've had all the ideas, you know. And it's your house that's crowded after all."

Edna was right. She didn't have any better ideas, so she had no business complaining. She may as well keep biting the bullet, or rather bullets. There were lots of them. She should just sit back and bite bullet one: her best friend now had another best friend. Bullet two: Rudy and her mother would get divorced. Bullet three: Alyce would live with them forever. Bullet four (or was it still bullet three?): she would never have her blue and white room to herself again. She'd never be Caroline. She'd be Angel the unhappy. Angel the sad. Angel the friendless. Angel the orphan. Tears ran over her eyelashes and down her cheeks.

Edna was putting grass down the back of Fendell's shirt. He was pretending it was tickling him and waving his arms, giggling. For the third time in just a few days, Angel ran into the house and threw herself in Alyce's beanbag chair.

Downstairs the phone was ringing. It kept on and on. Why didn't someone answer it? Surely there were enough people around to answer the phone!

At last she heard her mother pick it up. She couldn't hear what she said. But Angel knew it was more bad news. More company. A farewell from Rudy. (He could at least say good-bye in person and maybe leave some food money to last until her mom could get a job.) Or maybe it was a teacher at school saying they had made a mistake and Angel really had failed a grade and would not be going on. Another phone call, another bullet.

Once her grandma had read her a poem about losing things. Watches and keys and even people and friends. Even best friends. And the poem said none of the things lost were disasters. Angel always remembered it, but she didn't believe it. Her life was a disaster from all these losses.

"Angel?" said a voice close to her. She sat up. It was her mother.

"I thought I heard you crying! What in the world is the matter?"

It was too much, too long, too complicated. How could she answer the question? *Everything* was wrong!

"Do you know who was on the phone just now?"

Angel shook her head. Why did it matter?

"It was Alyce's landlord."

Oh, great, the apartment would take ten more years to fix. Or be rented out to someone else. Someone more dependable.

"Guess what he said! He said Alyce's apartment is ready for her to move back to anytime. Right away! It didn't take as long as they thought. He was able to get a couple of extra men to help."

Angel was afraid to stop crying. She was afraid to not be unhappy. The other shoe was bound to drop, and when it did she wanted to be ready.

"I, for one, will be glad that she's moving, won't you, Angel? I mean, I know we love her dearly, but living together is not easy. And I

113

know you have made the biggest sacrifice."

"No, I didn't," Angel heard herself say. She wanted to say, *you* did. You are the one who had no privacy, who lost her husband to Janet. No, the problem was not over. It was just beginning.

"What's going on up here?" called Rudy, coming into the room.

How could Rudy be home from work already? Had the whole afternoon gone by? Rudy gave his wife a kiss. She kissed him back.

"Alyce's apartment is ready!" said Angel's mother to her maybe-husband.

"What?" shouted Rudy. "Really?"

Rudy grabbed his wife around the waist, picked her up, and swung her over his head. Then he began to dance and sing around Angel's blue and white room, weaving in and out of Alyce's dangling pantyhose and face products. They began to laugh and giggle like Edna and Fendell. Her dad was girl crazy! Her mom was boy crazy! They were in love!

The two of them threw themselves on Angel's bed and hugged and kissed. They did not look like a couple who would divorce in the near future.

"We'll have our privacy back! And our souvlaki and our roast turkey and our house and children!" said Rudy. "Not that we don't love Alyce, you understand," he said quickly to Angel.

"My kitchen will be my own," said her mother. "The pet hair will be gone. The canary feathers won't be in my cereal. Not that I don't love Alyce," she said quickly. "You know we love her, Angel."

Angel did know. Angel even began to love her now that she knew Alyce was leaving. She hoped her parents would not be so hasty about letting people move in again. But they probably would because that's the kind of people they were. But at least there would be some time between guests. Time to forget.

"Then you aren't getting a divorce?" said Angel.

116

Her parents sat up on the bed. They stared at her. "Pardon me?" they said in unison. "What makes you say that?"

"You fought," said Angel, crying all over again. "And Janet."

"Janet?" they both said together. They sounded like a chorus!

Rudy gave Angel a hug. "We will always be married, Angel. It's a commitment. No argument or person could change that. We are a family. Do you understand that?"

Angel nodded. "Was it my...imagination again?"

They nodded. "Next time, Angel, come to us and ask. Don't keep things inside and suffer about them. We all were a little irritable with Alyce here, but all that means is that we were irritable," said her mother.

"And Janet...what in the world does she have to do with it?" asked Rudy.

Angel explained.

It looked as if her mom and dad wanted to

laugh but didn't. Their faces got red and they squeezed their mouths shut, and Rudy said, "Janet isn't interested in marriage or children. She wants a big career in New York. Not everyone is interested in marriage, no matter what Edna might tell you. But if she *did* want me because I was so tall and handsome and an all-around nice guy, she couldn't get to first base because I've got a wife and I've got a family, and all I need is one. And you're it."

"Hey, where are you guys? I'm hungry!" said Rags, coming into the room with dirt from his city on his hands. "I wish Mom would cook instead of Alyce or Clifford."

"Well, then, you're in luck, old boy, because that is just what's going to happen from now on." Rudy clapped him on the back.

"Yoo-hoo!" called Alyce, coming up the steps with Thena. It was getting crowded in Angel's room. They each had a big prune Danish, and Alyce handed her mother a bag with some for them.

"Before supper?" said Rudy. "We have got to get some order in this house!"

"And we will," said Mrs. Poppadopolis. "Alyce, I have some news I think you'll like! Your apartment is ready. You can move back in right away!"

"And we'll help you," said Rudy. "Tomorrow morning!"

"Oh, my," said Alyce with a frown. "I have an appointment at the hairdresser's in the morning."

"Cancel it," said Rudy, more firmly than necessary, Angel thought.

"It will be nice to be home," said Alyce. "But of course I'll miss you all so much, my little darlings!" She hugged Thena and Rags and Angel.

"No, they are *our* little darlings, just so you don't get confused," said Rudy.

Rudy was serious, but Alyce laughed because she thought he was joking.

"Well, I'll have to pack," said Alyce. "Of

course, we don't have to do it all at once, I mean I can move a box a day over time— "

"No, I think we'll do it all at once," said Angel's mother. "It's best that way."

FIFTEEN

The Rainbow after the Storm

Just then Edna and Fendell burst in the door of Angel's bedroom.

Alyce handed each of them a prune Danish.

"We couldn't find you!" said Edna to Angel. "I guess everyone is home from *work* already."

"A penny saved is a penny *earned*," said Fendell, which didn't seem connected to anything, thought Angel. Besides, they didn't need to think about S.P. ever again! She couldn't wait to tell her friends the news! For a moment she forgot all about being jealous.

Now it really *was* crowded in the bedroom!

"I think if we are going to meet like this, we should do it downstairs!" said Rudy. "Bedrooms aren't good for meetings. There aren't enough chairs!"

Everyone trooped down the stairs eating prune Danishes before supper. Angel knew things would be back in order soon, and there would be a routine and a schedule, and meals would be on time, and they would not burn, and no one would eat doughnuts before dinner.

On the way downstairs, Rudy whispered in Angel's ear, "Caroline, I'm so proud of you for biting the bullet and handling all those worries by yourself."

Angel didn't know she had handled the worries. They were just there; there was nothing to do about them.

"Bullets," said Angel. They may as well be accurate. There was more than one.

Rudy laughed. "That makes me even more proud," he said. "We'll get your room back in shape right away. We'll get rid of the cat hair and dog hair and pantyhose and feathers. Pretty soon, you'll be saying, 'Alyce who?'"

When they got downstairs, Rudy brought up a big box from the basement and handed it to Alyce. "No time like the present," he said. "Start packing!" Alyce laughed but took the box and went back up the stairs.

"Pack the sack! Pack the sack!" sang Rags.

Rudy started putting dog and cat food and brushes and collars into another box. Angel's mother went to the kitchen, where she was happy to start supper even though she knew no one was hungry.

"*Pssst!*" said Edna. "Let's go out on the porch. Fendell has this great new idea!"

"We don't need it!" said Angel. "Alyce is leaving."

Sitting on the swing, she told them all about it.

"Wow," said Fendell. "Well, it's just in time, because my dad and I are leaving too. School starts next week, and my dad sold cookware to almost everyone in Elm City. He said we have to move on."

"But he'll come and see us next summer," said Edna, "because his dad is thinking of a new line of herbs and spices that are organically grown."

Edna didn't seem upset that Fendell was leaving, thought Angel. He'd be gone all year, and in fact he might never come back. There was no mention of e-mail or letters or phone calls.

Edna said, "Well, I'm glad that's over! Now we can forget about Alyce and get ready for school. I want one of those new fake-fur jackets. They're really cool."

"Hey, they're not cool, they're warm!" said Fendell. "You don't want cool in Wisconsin! You want warm!"

"Ho, ho, ho," said Edna, but her heart wasn't in it. She made a face as if he wasn't all that funny. Edna was fickle! A few days ago she had laughed uproariously at his jokes. Some things Angel would never understand.

"Well, I've got to go," said Fendell. "I'll see you guys before we leave town."

"So long," said Edna.

"Thanks for all the help with Alyce," said Angel.

"It's been a fun summer," said Fendell.

Angel couldn't quite agree; it was more like work and worry, but she didn't want to split hairs, as her grandma said.

When Fendell was gone, Edna got a piece of paper and a pencil and wrote down what she wanted to buy for school.

"Here is your column," she said, drawing a line down the middle. "Should we both get fake-fur jackets? In different colors? Then everyone will know we are best friends."

"Are we best friends?" asked Angel.

Edna looked at her. "Of course," she said. "Why wouldn't we be?"

"Well, you were flirting with Fendell, like *he* was your best friend."

Edna sighed. "We can have more than one

friend, you know. I like to flirt, and I want a boyfriend. You will too." Then she added, "Someday. We can have other friends, Angel, and all go out together. That doesn't mean we aren't *best* friends."

So a person could flirt or have lunch with another clown, and it didn't mean anything! Nothing! She and Edna were still best friends. Her mom and Rudy were still married. Forever. There was so much to learn. And of course her imagination always got in the way.

When Alyce brought down her filled box, Rudy handed her an empty one. At this rate she'd be out of there tomorrow! Her mom peeled potatoes and put them in cold water to wait while she vacuumed up pet hair in the living room.

Before supper most of Alyce's belongings were packed.

"It feels like we are rushing her out," said Angel.

"We are," said Rudy.

Edna and Angel sat on the porch swing and watched the sun go behind the trees.

"It gets dark early now," said Angel.

"The days are shorter," said Edna. "Winter's coming."

"We can slide down the hill behind the church."

"And skate at the rink in the park."

The sky turned pink and rosy, and rays spread out of the setting sun like a picture on a greeting card. It was almost like a rainbow after a storm, thought Angel.

"We're going to take a few boxes over to Alyce's before supper, Angel," said Rudy. "Want to come?"

Angel shook her head.

"Maybe you can keep an eye on Thena then. She's in her playpen," said Mrs. Poppadopolis. "We'll just be a few minutes."

Angel nodded.

As Rudy walked to the car with the boxes, the girls heard him give Alyce some advice.

"I don't want to interfere," he said, "but if I were you, I'd use the oven a bit more instead of the grill, and keep your eye out for smoke. Where there's smoke there's..." Then the car door closed.

"...fire!" said the two girls together. They smiled.

"I think I'll eat at home tonight, Angel," said Edna. "I've had enough of Alyce today. Don't get me wrong. I like her and everything, I just don't want to eat with her again. Besides, I'm not very hungry after the prune Danish."

The girls began to laugh, and then they laughed harder, and pretty soon they couldn't stop. It was the way it used to be. Life was fun again, life was grand.

She still had a family. She had no bullets to bite. She had a best friend. And best of all, she had a room of her own with no pantyhose waiting to grab her.

When Edna left, Angel sat on the swing and felt sleepy. She heard her parents come into the

129

kitchen, laughing and talking. She heard Rags making up silly rhymes so his mom would praise him.

She heard Rudy say words that sounded like *exchange* and *student,* and *Greece.* Her mother's voice said phrases like *too soon to tell her, a year's a long time away,* and *sleep on it for now.*

As she nodded off, she murmured, "My wild imagination again. I have to do something about that real soon."

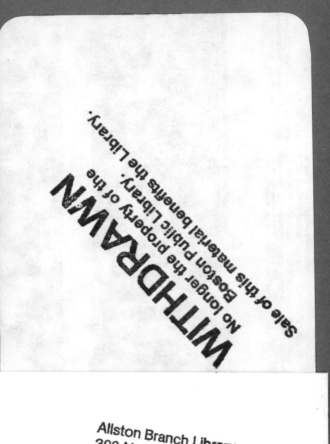